Dear Parent:

Congratulations! Your child is taking
the first steps on an exciting journey.
The destination? Independent reading!

STEP INTO READING® will help your child get there. The program offers
five steps to reading success. Each step includes fun stories and colorful art.
There are also Step into Reading Sticker Books, Step into Reading Math
Readers, Step into Reading Phonics Readers, Step into Reading Write-In
Readers, and Step into Reading Phonics Boxed Sets—a complete literacy
program with something for every child.

Learning to Read, Step by Step!

Ready to Read   Preschool–Kindergarten
• big type and easy words • rhyme and rhythm • picture clues
For children who know the alphabet and are eager to
begin reading.

Reading with Help   Preschool–Grade 1
• basic vocabulary • short sentences • simple stories
For children who recognize familiar words and sound out
new words with help.

Reading on Your Own   Grades 1–3
• engaging characters • easy-to-follow plots • popular topics
For children who are ready to read on their own.

Reading Paragraphs   Grades 2–3
• challenging vocabulary • short paragraphs • exciting stories
For newly independent readers who read simple sentences
with confidence.

Ready for Chapters   Grades 2–4
• chapters • longer paragraphs • full-color art
For children who want to take the plunge into chapter books
but still like colorful pictures.

STEP INTO READING® is designed to give every child a successful
reading experience. The grade levels are only guides. Children can progress
through the steps at their own speed, developing confidence in their
reading, no matter what their grade.

Remember, a lifetime love of reading starts with a single step!

To my grandsons,
Cole and Chase, with love
—T.R.

Step into Reading, Random House, and the Random House colophon are registered trademarks of Random House, Inc.

Visit us on the Web!
StepIntoReading.com
randomhouse.com/kids

Educators and librarians, for a variety of teaching tools, visit us at RHTeachersLibrarians.com

ISBN 978-0-7364-3119-4 (trade) — ISBN 978-0-7364-8130-4 (lib. bdg.)

Printed in the United States of America   25 24

Disney FROZEN

BIG SNOWMAN, LITTLE SNOWMAN

By Tish Rabe

Illustrated by the Disney Storybook Artists

Random House 🏠 New York

HAPPY sister.

SAD sister.

At first,

Hans seems nice.

Elsa runs away.
She makes the
snow and ice!

Anna gets ON her horse.

Ride, Anna, ride!

Anna falls OFF.

It's cold outside.

Anna meets Kristoff.

His reindeer is Sven.

Kristoff goes IN . . .

then OUT again!

Anna and Kristoff
go, go, go!
Sven climbs FAST.

Anna climbs SLOW.

Elsa has a palace.

Anna enters FIRST.

Kristoff enters LAST.

Elsa freezes Anna
with an icy blast!

COLD Olaf dreams
of the HOT, HOT sun.

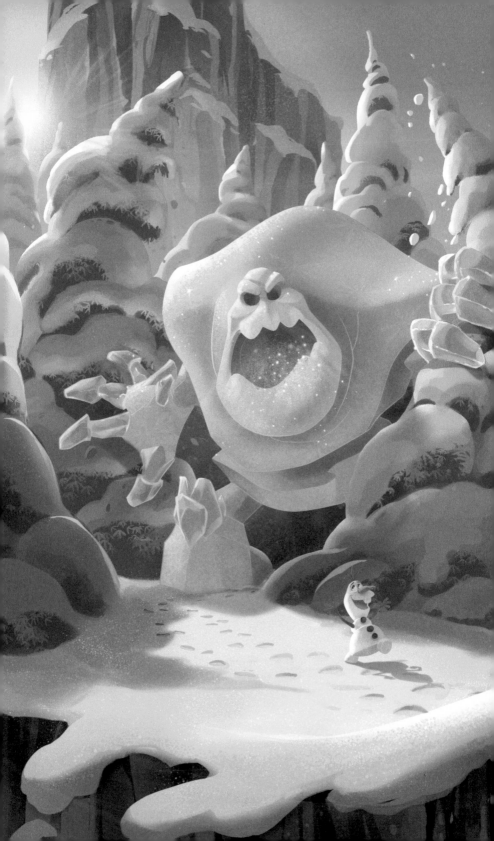

LITTLE snowman.

BIG snowman!

Run! Run! Run!

Anna is freezing.

She is worried, too.

She asks a troll
what to do.

Watch out!

Hans attacks!

Anna is in FRONT.

Elsa is in BACK.

Winter ENDS.

Summer STARTS.

Anna's act of love
has thawed
her frozen heart.

Olaf APART.

Sisters TOGETHER.

Elsa, Anna, and Olaf . . .

friends forever!